ROBERT E. HOWARD

PIGEONS FROM HELL

ADAPTED BY SCOTT HAMPTON

ECLIPSE BOOKS

ECLIPSE BOOKS, P. O. BOX 1099,
FORESTVILLE, CALIFORNIA 95436.
FIRST EDITION, NOVEMBER 1988.
TRADE PAPERBACK: ISBN 0-913035-
68-8. LIMITED EDITION, SIGNED
HARDCOVER: ISBN 0-913035-69-6.
"PIGEONS FROM HELL" © 1932, 1988
THE ESTATE OF ROBERT E.
HOWARD, GLENN LORD, EXECUTOR.
ADAPTATION AND PAINTINGS © 1988
SCOTT HAMPTON. INTRODUCTION ©
1988 RAMSEY CAMPBELL. THIS
BOOK WAS HAND—LETTERED BY
TRACY HAMPTON, EDITED BY
LETITIA GLOZER, AND DESIGNED
BY DEAN MULLANEY, WITH A
LOGOTYPE BY STEVE VANCE.

Dedicated to
Bo, Bunny, Robin,
Tracy, Toby, and Holly

INTRODUCTION

On learning that Robert E. Howard had committed suicide in 1936, H.P. Lovecraft wrote to E. Hoffman Price: "...for stark, living fear...the actual smell and feel and darkness and brooding horror and impending doom...what other writer is even in the running with REH? ...He was almost alone in his ability to create real emotions of fear and of dread suspense..."

Of Howard's relatively few horror stories, "Pigeons from Hell" best displays these qualities. Written in 1934 but published posthumously, it was suggested by stories told to Howard by his paternal grandmother Eliza. "All the gloominess and dark mysticism of the Gaelic nature were hers, and there was no light and mirth in her," he wrote to Lovecraft in 1930. "...In many of her tales...appeared the old, deserted plantation mansion, with the weeds growing rank about it and the ghostly pigeons flying up from the rails of the verandah."

The story has all the intensity and relentlessness of the nightmares that beset Howard since early childhood. May it also, like Frank Belknap Long's "The Space Eaters," have been an attempt by a friend and admirer to outdo Lovecraft for horror? While Long's tale contains a character modelled on Lovecraft himself, Howard's protagonist Griswell—"a lanky New Englander" given to cries of "My God! I must be mad"—would be more at home in Lovecraft's tales than in Howard's other work. (The sheriff Buckner, on the other hand—a Southerner who "would be a dangerous man in any sort of fight"—can be seen as one of Howard's idealized portraits of himself.) When Griswell admits "Witchcraft always meant the old towns of New England, to me—but all this is more terrible," one may sense Howard's triumph.

If the power of Howard's tale is worthy of Lovecraft, Scott Hampton's adaptation is worthy of Howard. Not only is it one of the most faithful and painstaking translations of a tale of terror into graphic form that I have ever seen, but it conjures all the atmosphere of oppressive decay and dread. As beautiful and subtle as it is horrifying, it is a triumph of its form.

Ramsey Campbell
Merseyside, England
22 September, 1988

GRISWELL AWOKE SUDDENLY, EVERY NERVE TINGLING WITH A PREMONITION OF IMMINENT PERIL.

HE STARED ABOUT WILDLY, UNABLE AT FIRST TO REMEMBER WHERE HE WAS, OR WHAT HE WAS DOING THERE. MOONLIGHT FILTERED IN THROUGH DUSTY WINDOWS, AND THE GREAT EMPTY ROOM WITH ITS LOFTY CEILING AND GAPING BLACK FIREPLACE WAS SPECTRAL AND UNFAMILIAR. THEN, AS HE EMERGED FROM THE CLINGING COBWEBS OF HIS RECENT SLEEP, HE REMEMBERED WHERE HE WAS AND HOW HE CAME TO BE THERE.

HE TWISTED HIS HEAD AND STARED AT HIS COMPANION, SLEEPING ON THE FLOOR NEAR HIM. JOHN BRANNER WAS BUT A VAGUELY BULKING SHAPE IN THE DARKNESS THAT THE MOON SCARCELY GRAYED.

NOW HE HAD CAPTURED THE ILLUSIVE MEMORY. IT WAS A DREAM, A NIGHTMARE SO FILLED WITH DIM TERROR THAT IT HAD FRIGHTENED HIM AWAKE. RECOLLECTION FLOODED BACK, VIVIDLY ETCHING THE ABOMINABLE VISION.

GRISWELL TRIED TO REMEMBER WHAT HAD AWAKENED HIM. THERE WAS NO SOUND IN THE HOUSE, NO SOUND OUTSIDE EXCEPT THE MOURNFUL HOOT OF AN OWL, FAR AWAY IN THE PINEY WOODS.

OR WAS IT A DREAM? CERTAINLY IT MUST HAVE BEEN, BUT IT HAD BLENDED SO CURIOUSLY WITH RECENT ACTUAL EVENTS THAT IT WAS DIFFICULT TO KNOW WHERE REALITY LEFT OFF AND FANTASY BEGAN.

DREAMING, HE HAD SEEMED TO RELIVE HIS PAST FEW WAKING HOURS IN ACCURATE DETAIL. THE DREAM HAD BEGUN ABRUPTLY, AS HE AND JOHN BRANNER CAME IN SIGHT OF THE HOUSE WHERE THEY NOW LAY.

THEY HAD COME RATTLING AND BOUNCING OVER THE STUMPY, UNEVEN OLD ROAD THAT LED THROUGH THE PINELANDS, HE AND JOHN BRANNER, WANDERING FAR AFIELD FROM THEIR NEW ENGLAND HOME IN SEARCH OF VACATION PLEASURE.

THEY HAD SIGHTED THE OLD HOUSE WITH ITS BALUSTRADED GALLERIES RISING AMIDST A WILDERNESS OF WEEDS AND BUSHES, JUST AS THE SUN WAS SETTING BEHIND IT. IT DOMINATED THEIR FANCY, REARING STARK AND GAUNT AGAINST THE LOW LURID RAMPART OF SUNSET, BARRED BY THE BLACK PINES.

THEY WERE TIRED, SICK OF BUMPING AND POUNDING ALL DAY OVER WOODLAND ROADS. THE OLD DESERTED HOUSE STIMULATED THEIR ARCHITECTS' IMAGINATION WITH ITS SUGGESTION OF ANTEBELLUM SPLENDOR AND ULTIMATE DECAY.

THEY LEFT THE AUTOMOBILE BESIDE THE RUTTY ROAD, AND AS THEY WENT UP THE WALK OF CRUMBLING BRICKS, ALMOST LOST IN THE TANGLE OF RANK GROWTH, PIGEONS ROSE FROM THE BALUSTRADES IN A FLUTTERING, FEATHERY CROWD AND SWEPT AWAY WITH A LOW THUNDER OF BEATING WINGS.

THE OAKEN DOOR SAGGED ON BROKEN HINGES. DUST LAY THICK ON THE FLOOR OF THE WIDE, DIM HALLWAY, ON THE BROAD STEPS OF THE STAIR THAT MOUNTED UP FROM THE HALL.

THEY TURNED INTO A DOOR OPPOSITE THE LANDING, AND ENTERED A LARGE ROOM, EMPTY, DUSTY, WITH COBWEBS SHINING THICKLY IN THE CORNERS. DUST LAY THICK OVER THE ASHES IN THE GREAT FIREPLACE.

THEY DISCUSSED GATHERING WOOD AND BUILDING A FIRE, BUT DECIDED AGAINST IT; AS THE SUN SANK, DARKNESS CAME QUICKLY, THE THICK DARKNESS OF THE PINELANDS. THEY KNEW THAT RATTLESNAKES AND COPPERHEADS HAUNTED SOUTHERN FORESTS, AND THEY DID NOT CARE TO GO GROPING FOR FIREWOOD IN THE DARK.

THEY ATE FRUGALLY FROM TINS, THEN ROLLED IN THEIR BLANKETS FULLY CLAD BEFORE THE EMPTY FIREPLACE AND WENT INSTANTLY TO SLEEP.

THIS, IN PART, WAS WHAT GRISWELL HAD DREAMED. HE SAW AGAIN THE GAUNT HOUSE LOOMING STARK AGAINST THE CRIMSON SUNSET, SAW THE FLIGHT OF THE PIGEONS AS HE AND BRANNER CAME UP THE SHATTERED WALK. HE SAW THE DIM ROOM IN WHICH THEY PRESENTLY LAY, AND THE TWO FORMS THAT WERE HIMSELF AND HIS COMPANION LYING WRAPPED IN THEIR BLANKETS. THEN, FROM THAT POINT, HIS DREAM ALTERED SUBTLY, PASSED OUT OF THE REALM OF THE COMMONPLACE AND BECAME TINGED WITH FEAR.

HE WAS LOOKING INTO A VAGUE, SHADOWY CHAMBER, LIT BY THE GRAY LIGHT OF THE MOON WHICH STREAMED IN FROM SOME OBSCURE SOURCE, FOR THERE WAS NO WINDOW IN THAT ROOM. BUT IN THE GRAY LIGHT HE SAW THREE SILENT SHAPES HANGING SUSPENDED IN A ROW, AND THEIR STILL, GRAY OUTLINES WOKE CHILL HORROR IN HIS SOUL.

THERE WAS NO SOUND, NO WORD, BUT HE SENSED A PRESENCE OF FEAR AND LUNACY CROUCHING IN A DARK CORNER...

... ABRUPTLY HE WAS BACK IN THE DUSTY, HIGH-CEILINGED ROOM, BEFORE THE GREAT FIREPLACE.

HE WAS LYING IN HIS BLANKETS, STARING TENSELY THROUGH THE DIM DOOR AND ACROSS THE SHADOWY HALL, TO WHERE A BEAM OF MOONLIGHT FELL ACROSS THE BALUSTRADED STAIR, SOME SEVEN STEPS UP FROM THE LANDING. AND THERE WAS SOMETHING AT THE HEAD OF THE STAIRS, A BENT, MISSHAPEN, SHADOWY THING THAT NEVER MOVED FULLY INTO THE BEAM OF LIGHT.

BUT A DIM YELLOW BLUR THAT MIGHT HAVE BEEN A FACE WAS TURNED TOWARD HIM AS IF *SOMETHING* CROUCHED ON THE STAIR REGARDING HIM AND HIS COMPANION.

FRIGHT CREPT THROUGH HIS VEINS AND IT WAS THEN THAT HE AWOKE --IF INDEED HE HAD BEEN ASLEEP.

HE BLINKED HIS EYES.

THE BEAM OF MOONLIGHT FELL ACROSS THE STAIR JUST AS HE HAD DREAMED IT DID, BUT NO FIGURE LURKED THERE.

THEN IT BEGAN...

...THE WHISTLING.

EERIE AND SWEET, IT DESCENDED ON THEM FROM THE FLOOR ABOVE, NOT CARRYING ANY TUNE, BUT PIPING SHRILL AND MELODIOUS.

SUCH A SOUND IN A SUPPOSEDLY DESERTED HOUSE WAS ALARMING ENOUGH, BUT IT WAS MORE THAN THE FEAR OF A PHYSICAL INVADER THAT HELD GRISWELL FROZEN.

HE COULD NOT HIMSELF HAVE DEFINED THE HORROR THAT GRIPPED HIM.

BRANNER'S BLANKETS RUSTLED AND GRISWELL SAW HE WAS SITTING UPRIGHT.

AND HE WAS LISTENING.

MORE SWEETLY AND MORE SUBTLY EVIL ROSE THAT WEIRD WHISTLING.

HE HAD MEANT TO SHOUT--TO TELL BRANNER THAT THERE WAS SOMEBODY UPSTAIRS, SOMEBODY WHO COULD MEAN THEM NO GOOD-- THAT THEY MUST LEAVE THE HOUSE AT ONCE. BUT HIS VOICE DIED DRYLY IN HIS THROAT.

BRANNER HAD RISEN. HIS BOOTS CLUMPED ON THE FLOOR AS HE MOVED TOWARD THE DOOR. HE STALKED LEISURELY INTO THE HALL AND MADE FOR THE LOWER LANDING, MERGING WITH THE SHADOWS THAT CLUSTERED BLACK ABOUT THE STAIR.

GRISWELL LAY INCAPABLE OF MOVEMENT, HIS MIND A WHIRL OF BEWILDERMENT. WHO WAS THAT WHISTLING UPSTAIRS?

GRISWELL SAW HIM CROSS THE SPOT WHERE THE MOON-LIGHT RESTED, SAW HIS HEAD TILTED BACK AS IF HE WERE LOOKING AT SOMETHING GRISWELL COULD NOT SEE, ABOVE AND BEYOND THE STAIR.

HE MOVED ACROSS THE BAR OF MOONLIGHT AND VANISHED FROM GRISWELL'S VIEW EVEN AS THE LATTER TRIED TO SHOUT TO HIM TO COME BACK. A GHASTLY WHISPER WAS THE ONLY RESULT OF HIS EFFORT.

THE WHISTLING SANK TO A LOWER NOTE, DIED OUT.

NOW HE HAD REACHED THE HALLWAY ABOVE. DEBRIS FALLING FROM ROTTED CEILING TIMBERS AND THE SOUND OF FLOORBOARDS CREAKING UNDER HIS MEASURED TREAD MARKED BRANNER'S PASSAGE.

SUDDENLY THE FOOTFALLS HALTED, AND THE WHOLE NIGHT SEEMED TO HOLD ITS BREATH.

THEN AN AWFUL SCREAM SPLIT THE STILLNESS, AND GRISWELL STARTED UP, ECHOING THE CRY.

THE STRANGE PARALYSIS THAT HAD HELD HIM WAS BROKEN. HE TOOK A STEP TOWARD THE DOOR, THEN CHECKED HIMSELF.

THE FOOTFALLS WERE RESUMED. BRANNER WAS COMING BACK.

HE WAS NOT RUNNING.

THE TREAD WAS EVEN MORE DELIBERATE AND MEASURED THAN BEFORE.

NOW THE STAIRS BEGAN TO CREAK AGAIN. A GROPING HAND, MOVING ALONG THE BALUSTRADE, CAME INTO THE BAR OF MOONLIGHT;

THEN ANOTHER, AND A GHASTLY THRILL WENT THROUGH GRISWELL AS HE SAW THAT THE OTHER HAND GRIPPED A HATCHET —

—A HATCHET WHICH DRIPPED BLACKLY. *WAS* THAT BRANNER WHO WAS COMING DOWN THE STAIR?

YES! THE FIGURE HAD MOVED INTO THE BAR OF MOONLIGHT NOW, AND GRISWELL RECOGNIZED IT. THEN HE SAW BRANNER'S FACE, AND A SHRIEK BURST FROM GRISWELL'S LIPS. BRANNER'S FACE WAS BLOODLESS, CORPSE-LIKE; GOUTS OF BLOOD DRIPPED DARKLY DOWN IT; HIS EYES WERE GLASSY AND WET, AND BLOOD OOZED FROM THE GREAT GASH...

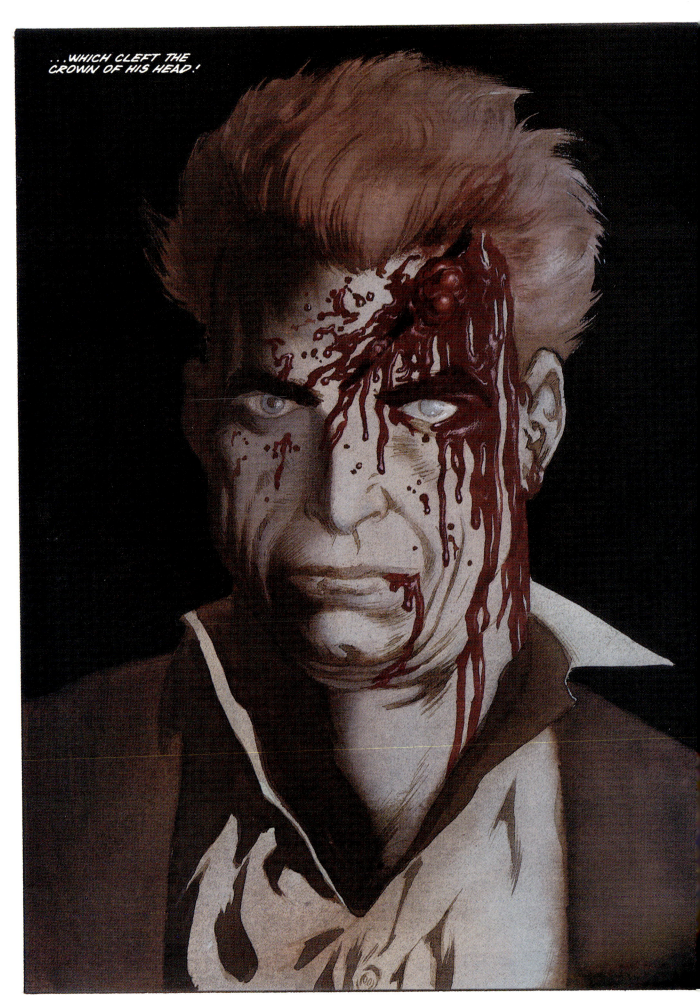

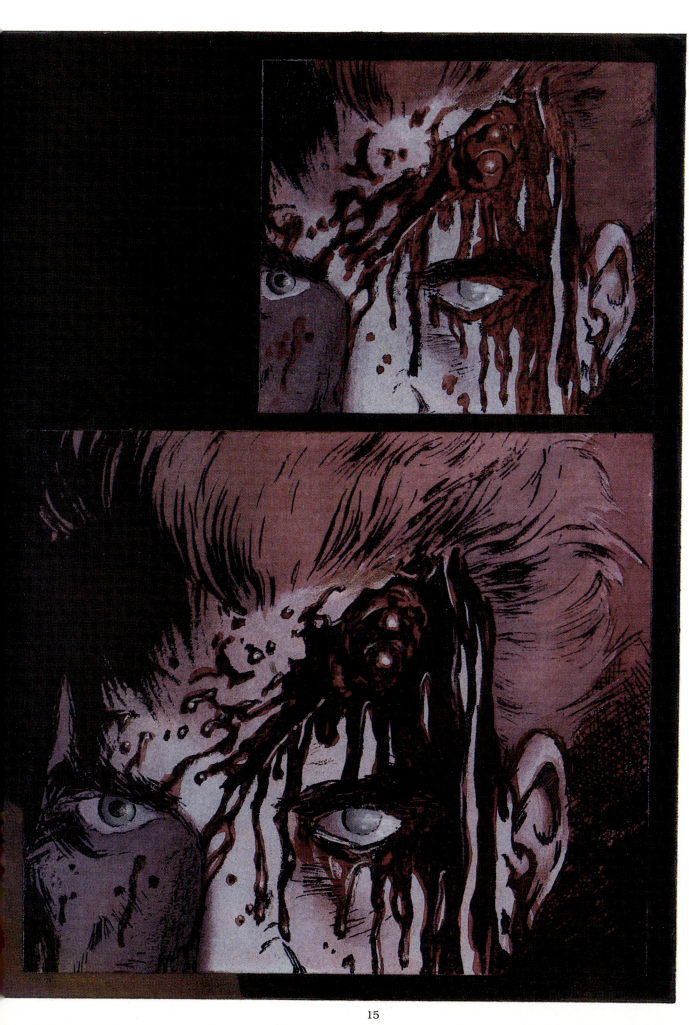

GRISWELL NEVER REMEMBERED EXACTLY HOW HE GOT OUT OF THAT ACCURSED HOUSE. AFTERWARD HE RETAINED A MAD, CONFUSED IMPRESSION OF SMASHING HIS WAY THROUGH A DUSTY COBWEBBED WINDOW, OF STUMBLING BLINDLY ACROSS THE WEED-CHOKED LAWN, GIBBERING HIS FRANTIC HORROR.

SOME SHRED OF SANITY RETURNED TO HIM AS HE SAW THE AUTOMOBILE BESIDE THE ROAD. IN A WORLD GONE SUDDENLY MAD, THAT WAS AN OBJECT REFLECTING PROSAIC REALITY. BUT EVEN AS HE REACHED FOR THE DOOR...

...A CHILLING WHIR SOUNDED IN HIS EARS, AND HE RECOILED FROM THE SWAYING, UNDULATING SHAPE THAT ARCHED UP FROM ITS COILS, DARTING A FORKED TONGUE IN THE MOONLIGHT.

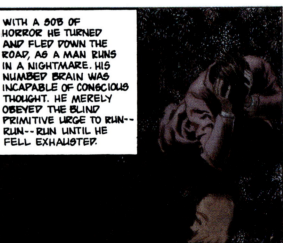

WITH A SOB OF HORROR HE TURNED AND FLED DOWN THE ROAD, AS A MAN RUNS IN A NIGHTMARE. HIS NUMBED BRAIN WAS INCAPABLE OF CONSCIOUS THOUGHT. HE MERELY OBEYED THE BLIND PRIMITIVE URGE TO RUN-- RUN-- RUN UNTIL HE FELL EXHAUSTED.

THE BLACK PINES FLOWED END-LESSLY PAST HIM; SO HE WAS SEIZED WITH THE ILLUSION THAT HE WAS GETTING NOWHERE. BUT PRESENTLY A SOUND PENETRATED THE FOG OF HIS TERROR...

...THE STEADY, INEXORABLE PATTER OF FEET BEHIND HIM.

TURNING HIS HEAD, HE SAW *SOMETHING* LOPING AFTER HIM--WOLF OR DOG, HE COULD NOT TELL WHICH, BUT ITS EYES GLOWED LIKE BALLS OF GREEN FIRE.

WITH A GASP HE INCREASED HIS SPEED, REELED AROUND A BEND IN THE ROAD, AND HEARD A HORSE SNORT, SAW IT REAR AND HEARD ITS RIDER CURSE, SAW THE GLEAM OF BLUE STEEL IN THE MAN'S LIFTED HAND.

FOR GOD'S SAKE, HELP ME! THE THING! IT KILLED BRANNER--IT'S COMING AFTER ME!!

LOOK!!

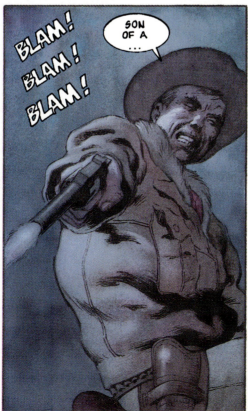

BLAM! BLAM! BLAM!

SON OF A ...

BLAM! BLAM!

BLAM! CLICK!

CLICK!

THE FIRE SPARKS VANISHED, AND THE RIDER, JERKING HIS STIRRUP FREE FROM GRISWELL'S GRASP, SPURRED HIS HORSE TO THE BEND.

TOOK TO THE BRUSH. TIMBER WOLF, I FIGURE, THOUGH I NEVER HEARD OF ONE CHASING A MAN BEFORE.

WHAT'S ALL THIS ABOUT, ANYWAY?

ARE YOU AFRAID TO GO BACK TO THE HOUSE?

THE THOUGHT OF FACING THAT HORROR AGAIN TURNS ME SICK. BUT POOR BRANNER --

--WE HAVE TO FIND HIS BODY.

MY GOD! *WHAT* WILL WE FIND? IF A DEAD MAN WALKS, WHAT --

WE'LL SEE.

AS THEY MADE THE TURN, GRISWELL'S BLOOD WAS ICE AT THE THOUGHT OF WHAT THEY MIGHT SEE LUMBERING UP THE ROAD WITH A BLOODY, GRINNING DEATH-MASK, BUT THEY SAW ONLY THE HOUSE LOOMING SPECTRALLY AMONG THE PINES, DOWN THE ROAD.

GOD, HOW EVIL THAT HOUSE LOOKS FROM THE VERY FIRST--WHEN WE SAW THOSE PIGEONS FLY UP FROM THE PORCH.

PIGEONS?

YOU SAW THE PIGEONS?

DOZENS-- PERCHING ON THE PORCH RAILING.

I'VE LIVED IN THIS COUNTRY ALL MY LIFE. I'VE PASS-ED THE OLD BLASSENVILLE PLACE A THOUSAND TIMES, I RECKON, AT ALL HOURS OF THE DAY AND NIGHT. BUT I NEVER SAW A PIGEON ANYWHERE AROUND IT, OR ANY-WHERE ELSE IN THESE WOODS.

THERE WERE SCORES OF THEM.

SOME FOLKS SAY THEY'VE SEEN THE PIGEONS, BUT NOBODY HEREABOUTS WILL PASS ALONG THIS ROAD BETWEEN SUNDOWN AND SUNUP. THEY SAY THE PIGEONS ARE THE BLASSENVILLES, LET OUT OF HELL AT SUNSET.

WHO WERE THE BLASSENVILLES?

THEY OWNED ALL THIS LAND HERE. FRENCH-ENGLISH FAMILY. CAME HERE FROM THE WEST INDIES BEFORE THE LOUISIANA PURCHASE. THE CIVIL WAR RUINED THEM, LIKE IT DID SO MANY. SOME WERE KILLED IN THE WAR. MOST OF THE OTHERS DIED OUT. NOBODY'S LIVED IN THE MANOR SINCE 1890.

WELL, NOW-- THAT'S A *PRETTY* LITTLE THING. SHE YOURS?

THIS YOUR AUTO?

SORRY. YES. BE CAREFUL. THERE'S A SNAKE ON THE SEAT--OR THERE WAS.

NOT THERE NOW.

WELL, LET'S HAVE A LOOK.

THE OAKEN DOOR SAGGED AS IT HAD BEFORE. BUCKNER LED THE WAY--TORCH IN ONE HAND, GUN IN THE OTHER.

AS HE SWUNG HIS LIGHT INTO THE ROOM ACROSS FROM THE STAIRWAY, GRISWELL CRIED OUT, ALMOST FAINTING WITH THE INTOLERABLE SICK-NESS AT WHAT HE SAW.

22

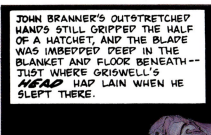

JOHN BRANNER'S OUTSTRETCHED HANDS STILL GRIPPED THE HALF OF A HATCHET, AND THE BLADE WAS IMBEDDED DEEP IN THE BLANKET AND FLOOR BENEATH-- JUST WHERE GRISWELL'S *HEAD* HAD LAIN WHEN HE SLEPT THERE.

GRISWELL, IF YOU'RE HOLD-IN' BACK ANYTHING, YOU BETTER SPILL IT. GIVE ME THE STRAIGHT GOODS NOW AND IT'LL MAKE IT EASIER.

WASN'T IT SOMETHING LIKE THIS: YOU QUARRELED, HE GRABBED A HATCHET AND SWUNG AT YOU, BUT YOU DODGED AND THEN LET *HIM* HAVE IT?

GREAT GOD, MAN, *I* DIDN'T MUR-DER JOHN! WE WERE *BEST FRIENDS!*

I DON'T BLAME YOU FOR NOT BELIEVING ME. BUT... GOD HELP ME, IT IS THE *TRUTH!*

HMM...

I BELIEVE THIS HATCHET IN HIS HANDS IS THE ONE HE WAS KILLED WITH. BLOOD AND BRAINS PLASTERED ON THE BLADE, AND HAIRS STICKIN' TO IT--HAIRS EXACTLY THE SAME COLOR AS HIS. THIS MAKES IT TOUGH FOR YOU, GRISWELL.

HOW SO?

KNOCK ANY PLEA OF SELF-DEFENSE IN THE HEAD. BRANNER COULDN'T HAVE SWUNG AT YOU WITH THIS HATCHET AFTER YOU SPLIT HIS SKULL WITH IT. YOU MUST HAVE PULLED THE AX OUT OF HIS HEAD, STUCK IT INTO THE FLOOR AND CLAMPED HIS FINGERS ON IT TO MAKE IT LOOK LIKE HE'D ATTACKED YOU, AND IT WOULD HAVE BEEN DAMNED CLEVER--IF YOU'D USED ANOTHER HATCHET.

I DIDN'T KILL HIM! I HAVE NO INTENTION OF PLEADING SELF-DEFENSE.

THAT'S WHAT PUZZLES ME; WHAT MUR-DERER WOULD RIG UP SUCH A CRAZY STORY TO PROVE HIS INNOCENCE?

AVERAGE KILLER WOULD HAVE TOLD A LOGICAL YARN, AT LEAST.

23

HMMM! BLOOD DROPS LEADIN' FROM THE DOOR. THE BODY WAS DRAGGED-- NO, COULDN'T HAVE BEEN DRAGGED; THE FLOOR ISN'T SMEARED. YOU MUST HAVE CARRIED IT HERE, AFTER KILLIN' HIM IN SOME OTHER PLACE. BUT, IN THAT CASE, WHY ISN'T THERE ANY BLOOD ON YOUR CLOTHES? OF COURSE, YOU CHANGED YOUR CLOTHES AND WASHED YOUR HANDS. BUT THE FELLOW HASN'T BEEN DEAD LONG.

HE WALKED DOWNSTAIRS AND ACROSS THE ROOM! HE STRUCK WHERE I WOULD HAVE BEEN IF I *HADN'T AWAKENED!*

THAT WINDOW-- I BURST *OUT* OF IT! YOU SEE IT'S BROKEN!

YEAH, I SEE.

THE BLOOD DROPS LEAD IN HERE. COME ON. WE'LL FOLLOW THEM.

THEY LEAD UPSTAIRS.

ARE YOU AFRAID TO GO UP THERE WITH ME?

YES. BUT I'M GOING WITH OR WITHOUT YOU. THE THING THAT KILLED JOHN MAY STILL BE HIDING UP THERE.

STAY BEHIND ME. IF ANYTHING JUMPS US, I'LL TAKE CARE OF IT. BUT FOR YOUR OWN SAKE, I WARN YOU THAT I SHOOT QUICKER'N A CAT JUMPS, AND I DON'T TEND TO MISS. IF YOU'RE THINKIN' ABOUT LAYIN' ME OUT FROM BEHIND, FORGET IT.

DON'T BE A *FOOL!*

RESENTMENT GOT THE BETTER OF GRISWELL'S APPREHENSION, AND THIS OUTBURST SEEMED TO REASSURE BUCKNER MORE THAN ANY OF HIS PROTESTATIONS OF INNOCENCE.

I WANT TO BE FAIR. IF ONLY HALF OF WHAT YOU'RE TELLING ME IS TRUE, YOU'VE BEEN THROUGH A HELL OF A LOT AND I DON'T WANT TO BE TOO HARD ON YOU. BUT YOU CAN SEE IT'S A CHUNK TO SWALLOW.

NOW, THEN...

THEY CAME OUT INTO THE UPPER HALLWAY, A VAST, EMPTY SPACE OF DUST AND SHADOWS WHERE TIME-CRUSTED WINDOWS REPELLED THE MOONLIGHT AND THE GRAY RING OF BUCKNER'S TORCH SEEMED INADEQUATE. GRISWELL SHUDDERED; JOHN BRANNER HAD DIED HERE -- IN THE DARK.

26

BUT WITHOUT HASTE BUCKNER MADE HIS WAY TO THE STAIR AND BACKED DOWN IT, GRISWELL PRECEDING HIM, AND FIGHTING BLIND, MAD PANIC WITH EVERY STEP.

A GHASTLY THOUGHT BROUGHT ICY SWEAT OUT OF HIS FLESH.

SUPPOSE THE DEAD MAN WERE CREEPING UP THE STAIR BE-BEHIND THEM IN THE DARK, FACE FROZEN IN THE DEATH GRIN...

...BLOOD-CAKED HATCHET LIFTED TO STRIKE?

THIS POSSIBILITY SO OVERPOWERED HIM THAT HE WAS SCARCELY AWARE WHEN HIS FEET STRUCK THE LEVEL OF THE LOWER HALLWAY AND HE WAS ONLY THEN CONSCIOUS THAT THE LIGHT HAD GROWN BRIGHTER AS THEY DE-SCENDED, UNTIL IT NOW GLEAMED WITH FULL POWER.

THE DAMN THING WAS *CONJURED!* NOTHIN' ELSE. IT COULDN'T ACT LIKE THAT NATURALLY.

TURN THE LIGHT INTO THE ROOM. SEE IF... IF JOHN IS--

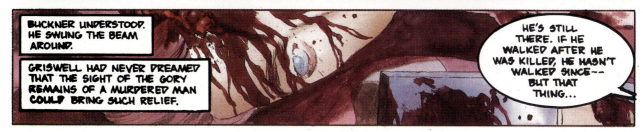

BUCKNER UNDERSTOOD. HE SWUNG THE BEAM AROUND.

GRISWELL HAD NEVER DREAMED THAT THE SIGHT OF THE GORY REMAINS OF A MURDERED MAN COULD BRING SUCH RELIEF.

HE'S STILL THERE. IF HE WALKED AFTER HE WAS KILLED, HE HASN'T WALKED SINCE-- BUT THAT THING...

AGAIN BUCKNER TURNED THE LIGHT UP THE STAIR, AND STOOD CHEWING HIS LIP AND SCOWLING. THREE TIMES HE HALF LIFTED HIS GUN. GRISWELL READ HIS MIND. THE SHERIFF WAS TEMPTED TO PLUNGE BACK UP THAT STAIR, TAKE HIS CHANCE WITH THE UNKNOWN. BUT COMMON SENSE HELD HIM BACK.

I WOULDN'T HAVE A CHANCE IN THE DARK, AND I'VE GOT A HUNCH THE LIGHT WOULD GO OUT AGAIN.

THERE'S NO USE DODGIN' THE QUESTION. THERE'S SOMETHIN' HELLISH IN THIS HOUSE, AND I THINK I HAVE AN INKLIN' OF WHAT IT IS. I DON'T BELIEVE YOU KILLED BRANNER. WHATEVER KILLED HIM IS UP THERE-- NOW.

I NEVER MET ANYTHING I WAS AFRAID TO TACKLE IN THE DARK BEFORE, BUT I'M NOT GOIN' UP THERE UNTIL DAYLIGHT. IT'S NOT LONG UNTIL DAWN. WE'LL WAIT OUT THERE ON THE PORCH.

THE STARS WERE ALREADY PALING WHEN THEY CAME OUT ON THE BROAD GALLERY. GRISWELL LEANED BACK AGAINST A CRUMBLING PILLAR AND SHUT HIS EYES, GRATEFUL FOR THE FAINT BREEZE THAT SEEMED TO COOL HIS THROBBING BRAIN.

HE EXPERIENCED A DULL SENSE OF UNREALITY. HE WAS A STRANGER IN A STRANGE LAND, A LAND THAT HAD BECOME SUDDENLY IMBUED WITH BLACK HORROR. THE SHADOW OF THE NOOSE HOVERED ABOVE HIM, AND IN THAT DARK HOUSE LAY JOHN BRANNER, WITH HIS BUTCHERED HEAD--LIKE THE FIGMENTS OF A DREAM THESE FACTS SPUN AND EDDIED IN HIS BRAIN UNTIL ALL MERGED IN A GRAY TWILIGHT AS SLEEP CAME UNINVITED TO HIS WEARY SOUL.

HE AWOKE TO A COLD WHITE DAWN AND FULL MEMORY OF THE HORRORS OF THE NIGHT. MISTS CURLED ABOUT THE STEMS OF THE PINES, CRAWLED IN SMOKY WISPS UP THE BROKEN WALK.

WAKE UP, GRISWELL. IT'S DAYLIGHT.

I'M READY. LET'S GO UPSTAIRS.

I'VE ALREADY BEEN. I DIDN'T WAKE YOU UP. I WENT AS SOON AS IT WAS LIGHT.

I FOUND NOTHIN'.

THE TRACKS OF THE BARE FEET--?

GONE. THE DUST HAD BEEN DISTURBED ALL OVER THE HALL FROM THE POINT WHERE BRANNER'S TRACKS ENDED--SWEPT INTO CORNERS. NO CHANCE OF FINDING ANYTHING THERE NOW.

SOMETHIN' OBLITERATED THOSE TRACKS AS WE SAT HERE, AND I DIDN'T HEAR A SOUND.

GRISWELL SHUDDERED AT THE THOUGHT OF HIMSELF SLEEPING ALONE ON THE PORCH WHILE BUCKNER CONDUCTED HIS EXPLORATION.

WHAT'LL WE DO? WITH THOSE TRACKS GONE THERE GOES MY ONLY CHANCE OF PROVING MY STORY.

WE'LL TAKE BRANNER'S BODY INTO THE COUNTY SEAT. LET ME DO THE TALKIN'. I DON'T BELIEVE YOU KILLED BRANNER, BUT NOBODY'LL BELIEVE WHAT YOU TOLD ME, OR WHAT HAPPENED TO US LAST NIGHT.

I'M HANDLIN' THIS THING MY WAY: I'LL SIMPLY TELL THE D.A. THAT JOHN BRANNER WAS KILLED BY A PARTY OR PARTIES UNKNOWN, AND THAT I'M WORKIN' ON THE CASE.

GRISWELL'S SOUL REVOLTED AT THE SIGHT OF JOHN BRANNER'S BLOODLESS FACE IN THE CHILL WHITE DAWN, THE FEEL OF HIS STIFFENING FLESH. THE GRAY FOG WRAPPED WISPY TENTACLES ABOUT THEIR LEGS AS THEY CARRIED THEIR GRISLY BURDEN ACROSS THE LAWN.

THE STRAIN OF THE DAY SPENT AT THE COUNTY SEAT WAS ADDED TO THE HORROR THAT STILL RODE GRISWELL'S SOUL LIKE THE SHADOW OF A BLACK-WINGED VULTURE. HE HAD NOT SLEPT, HADN'T TASTED WHAT HE HAD EATEN.

I TOLD YOU I'D TELL YOU ABOUT THE BLASSENVILLES.

THEY WERE PROUD FOLKS, HAUGHTY AND PRETTY DAMN RUTHLESS WHEN THEY WANTED THEIR WAY. THEY SAY WHEN A BLASSENVILLE DIED, THE DEVIL WAS ALWAYS WAITIN' FOR HIM OUT IN THE BLACK PINES.

"WELL, AFTER THE CIVIL WAR THEY DIED OFF PRETTY FAST, 'TIL FINALLY THERE WERE ONLY FOUR GIRLS LEFT ON THE OLD PLANTATION, THREE SISTERS AND THEIR OLDER COUSIN—WITH A FEW BLACKS WORKIN' THE FIELDS ON THE SHARE. THOSE GIRLS KEPT TO THEMSELVES. FOLKS DIDN'T SEE 'EM FOR MONTHS AT A TIME.

"BUT FOLKS KNEW ABOUT IT WHEN MISS CELIA CAME TO LIVE WITH THEM. SHE CAME FROM SOMEWHERE IN THE WEST INDIES, WHERE THE WHOLE FAMILY HAD ITS ROOTS--

"--A FINE, HANDSOME WOMAN, THEY SAY, IN HER EARLY THIRTIES. BUT SHE DIDN'T MIX WITH FOLKS ANY MORE THAN THE GIRLS DID. SHE BROUGHT A MULATTO MAID WITH HER, AND THE BLASSENVILLE CRUELTY CROPPED OUT IN HER TREATMENT OF THIS MAID.

"I KNEW AN OLD MAN, YEARS AGO, WHO SWORE HE SAW MISS CELIA TIE THIS GIRL UP TO A TREE, STARK NAKED, AND WHIP HER WITH A HORSEWHIP. NOBODY WAS SURPRISED WHEN SHE DISAPPEARED. EVERYBODY FIGURED SHE JUST RAN AWAY.

"ONE DAY, IN THE SPRING OF 1890, MISS ELIZABETH, THE YOUNGEST GIRL, CAME INTO TOWN FOR SUPPLIES.

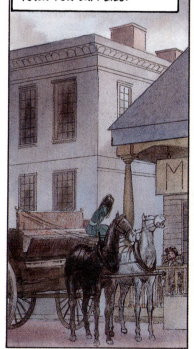

"WORD WAS SHE SEEMED A BIT WILD. MISS CELIA HAD GONE, WITHOUT LEAVING ANY WORD. SAID HER SISTERS THOUGHT SHE HAD GONE BACK TO THE WEST INDIES, BUT SHE BELIEVED HER AUNT WAS STILL IN THE HOUSE!

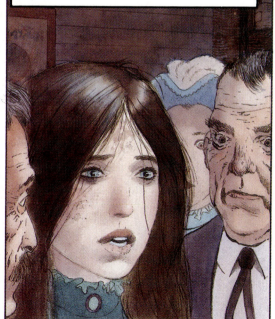

"SHE DIDN'T SAY WHAT SHE MEANT. JUST GOT HER SUPPLIES AND PULLED OUT FOR THE MANOR.

"IT WAS ABOUT A MONTH LATER WHEN MISS ELIZABETH CAME TEARIN' INTO TOWN NEARLY DEAD FROM FRIGHT. SHE FELL FROM HER HORSE IN THE SQUARE.

"WHEN SHE COULD TALK SHE SAID THE OTHER GIRLS HAD DISAPPEARED ONE BY ONE. FOR A WEEK SHE'D BEEN ALL ALONE AT THE MANOR.

"SHE'D BEEN AFRAID TO STAY THERE BUT DIDN'T KNOW WHERE ELSE TO GO. SHE'D BEEN LOCKIN' HERSELF IN HER ROOM AT NIGHT WITH CANDLES BURNIN'.

"EARLIER THAT NIGHT SHE'D FOUND A SECRET ROOM IN THE MANOR THAT HAD BEEN FORGOTTEN FOR A HUNDRED YEARS...

"...AND IN IT, HER COUSIN AND TWO SISTERS DEAD AND HANGIN' BY THEIR NECKS FROM THE CEILIN'.

"SHE SAID SOMEONE CHASED AND NEARLY BRAINED HER WITH AN AX AS SHE RAN OUT THE FRONT DOOR.

"SOMEONE OR *SOMETHING* WITH A YEL-LOW FACE."

"ABOUT A HUNDRED MEN RODE OUT THERE RIGHT AWAY. THEY SEARCHED THE HOUSE FROM TOP TO BOTTOM, BUT THEY DIDN'T FIND ANY SECRET ROOM, OR THE REMAINS OF THE SISTERS."

"BUT THEY *DID* FIND A HATCHET STICKIN' IN THE DOOR DOWNSTAIRS WITH SOME OF MISS ELIZABETH'S HAIRS STUCK ON IT, LIKE SHE'D SAID. SHE WOULDN'T GO BACK AND SHOW THEM HOW TO FIND THE SECRET DOOR-- WENT WILD WHEN THEY SUGGESTED IT."

WHEN SHE WAS ABLE TO TRAVEL, FOLKS LOANED HER SOME MONEY AND SHE WENT TO CALIFORNIA. SHE NEVER CAME BACK, BUT LATER IT WAS LEARNED, WHEN SHE SENT BACK TO REPAY THE MONEY, THAT SHE MARRIED OUT THERE.

AND THAT'S AS MUCH AS ANYONE KNOWS ABOUT THE BLASSENVILLES.

THEY DROVE ON IN SILENCE FOR A TIME, THEN BUCKNER WRENCHED THE WHEEL AROUND AND TURNED INTO A DIM TRACE THAT LEFT THE MAIN ROAD AND MEANDERED OFF THROUGH THE PINES.

WHERE ARE WE GOING?

THERE'S AN OLD VOODOO MAN LIVES DOWN HERE. I WANT TO TALK TO HIM. WE'RE UP AGAINST SOMETHIN' THAT TAKES MORE THAN WHITE MAN'S SENSE.

BUCKNER BROUGHT THE AUTOMOBILE TO A HALT IN A CLEARING WHERE THE ONLY EVIDENCE OF HUMAN HABITATION, A SMALL CABIN, SQUATTED IN THE SHADE OF HUGE OAKS AND CYPRESSES.

THERE HE IS. COME ON.

AN OLD MAN SAT SEPARATING MUSHROOMS AT THE FRINGE OF THE CLEARING. HE LOOKED UP AS THEY APPROACHED, BUT DID NOT RISE.

TIME'S COME FOR YOU TO TALK, JACOB.

YOU KNOW THE SECRET OF BLASSENVILLE MANOR. NOW, A MAN WAS MURDERED THERE LAST NIGHT AND THIS MAN HERE COULD HANG FOR IT UNLESS YOU TELL ME WHAT HAUNTS THAT OLD HOUSE.

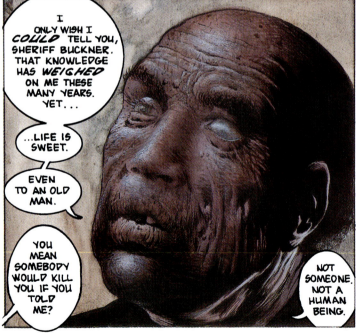

I ONLY WISH I COULD TELL YOU, SHERIFF BUCKNER. THAT KNOWLEDGE HAS WEIGHED ON ME THESE MANY YEARS. YET...

...LIFE IS SWEET.

EVEN TO AN OLD MAN.

YOU MEAN SOMEBODY WOULD KILL YOU IF YOU TOLD ME?

NOT SOMEONE. NOT A HUMAN BEING.

THE BIG SERPENT, THE BLACK GOD OF THE SWAMPS, GUARDS MY SECRET.

HE WOULD SEND A LITTLE BROTHER TO KISS ME WITH HIS COLD LIPS.

A LITTLE BROTHER WITH A WHITE CRESCENT MOON ON HIS HEAD.

36

JOAN WAS BEAUTIFUL-- I COULD NOT REFUSE HER.

JOAN.

WHAT IS A ZUVEMBIE, JACOB?

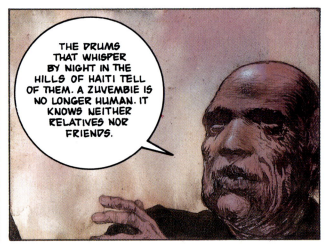

THE DRUMS THAT WHISPER BY NIGHT IN THE HILLS OF HAITI TELL OF THEM. A ZUVEMBIE IS NO LONGER HUMAN. IT KNOWS NEITHER RELATIVES NOR FRIENDS.

IT IS ONE WITH THE PEOPLE OF THE BLACK WORLD AND COMMANDS THE NATURAL DEMONS-- OWLS, BATS, SNAKES AND WEREWOLVES. A ZUVEMBIE THRIVES IN THE SHADOWS AND CAN FETCH DARKNESS TO BLOT OUT LIGHT.

IT CAN BE SLAIN BY LEAD OR STEEL. OTHERWISE IT LIVES FOREVER. TIME MEANS NAUGHT TO THE ZUVEMBIE; AN HOUR, A DAY, A YEAR, ALL IS ONE.

IT HYPNOTIZES THE LIVING BY THE SOUND OF ITS VOICE, AND WHEN IT SLAYS A MAN IT CAN COMMAND HIS LIFELESS BODY UNTIL THE FLESH IS COLD. AS LONG AS THE BLOOD FLOWS, THE CORPSE IS ITS SLAVE.

ITS PLEASURE LIES IN THE SLAUGHTER OF HUMAN BEINGS.

THIS IS ALL I KNOW, GENTLEMEN.

ONE MORE THING, JACOB-- WHY SHOULD ONE BECOME A ZUVEMBIE?

HATE! REVENGE! BUT JOAN . . .

THE SUN WAS HOVERING ABOVE THE HORIZON, VISIBLE IN DAZZLING RED FLAME THROUGH THE BLACK STEMS OF THE TREES, AS THE TWO MEN REGAINED THE ROAD.

YOU THINK IT'S THIS MULATTO GIRL, THIS JOAN, WHO KILLED BRANNER?

YOU HEARD WHAT OLD JACOB SAID -- TIME MEANS NOTHIN' TO A ZUVEMBIE.

AS THEY MADE THE LAST TURN IN THE ROAD, GRISWELL BRACED HIMSELF AGAINST THE SIGHT OF BLASSENVILLE MANOR LOOMING DARK AGAINST THE RED SUNSET. WHEN IT CAME INTO VIEW HE BIT HIS LIP TO KEEP FROM LOSING HIS WITS. THE SUGGESTION OF CRYPTIC HORROR CAME BACK IN ALL ITS POWER.

LOOK!

FROM THE BALLUSTRADES OF THE GALLERY ROSE A WHIRLING CLOUD OF PIGEONS THAT SWEPT AWAY INTO THE SOUTHERN TWILIGHT.

BOTH MEN SAT RIGID FOR A FEW MOMENTS AFTER THE PIGEONS HAD FLOWN.

WELL, NOW I'VE SEEN THEM.

MAYBE ONLY THE DOOMED SEE THEM.

WELL, WE'LL SEE.

COME ON.

AS THEY CAME INTO THE BROAD HALL GRISWELL SAW THE STRING OF BLACK SPOTS LEADING FROM THE STAIRS INTO THE CHAMBER, MARKING THE PATH OF A DEAD MAN.

I'LL LIE NEXT TO THIS DOOR, HERE. YOU LIE WHERE YOU DID LAST NIGHT.

SHALL WE LIGHT A FIRE IN THE GRATE?

NO. YOU'VE GOT A FLASHLIGHT AND SO DO I. WE'LL LIE HERE AND SEE WHAT HAPPENS. CAN YOU USE THAT GUN I GAVE YOU?

I'M NOT SURE. I SUPPOSE SO.

WELL, LEAVE THE SHOOTIN' TO ME, IF POSSIBLE. THERE'S NO MOON TONIGHT AND I DON'T WANT TO GET MY HEAD BLOWN OFF IN THE DARK.

YOU'RE NOT GOING TO USE YOUR FLASHLIGHT?

NO. I THINK WE NEED TO BE IN THE DARK-- LIKE YOU AND BRANNER WERE.

I'M GOING TO CUT IT OFF NOW. LET'S BEGIN OUR WATCH.

FEAR LIKE A PHYSICAL SICKNESS ASSAILED GRISWELL WHEN THE ROOM WAS PLUNGED IN DARKNESS. HE LAY TREMBLING AND HIS HEART BEAT SO HEAVILY HE FELT AS IF HE WOULD SUFFOCATE. TIME SEEMED AT A STANDSTILL. THE EFFORT HE MADE TO CONTROL HIS CRUMBLING NERVES BATHED HIS LIMBS IN SWEAT. HE CLENCHED HIS TEETH UNTIL HIS JAWS ACHED AND ALMOST LOCKED, AND THE NAILS OF HIS FINGERS BIT DEEPLY INTO HIS PALMS.

HE DID NOT KNOW WHAT HE WAS EXPECTING. THE FIEND WOULD STRIKE AGAIN--BUT HOW? WOULD IT BE A HORRIBLE, SWEET WHISTLING, BARE FEET STEALING DOWN THE CREAKING STEPS, OR A SUDDEN HATCHET-STROKE IN THE DARK? WOULD IT CHOOSE HIM OR BUCKNER? WAS BUCKNER *ALREADY DEAD?* HE COULD SEE NOTHING IN THE BLACKNESS, BUT HE HEARD THE MAN'S STEADY BREATHING.

OR *WAS* THAT BUCKNER BREATHING BESIDE HIM, SEPARATED BY A NARROW STRIP OF DARKNESS? HAD THE FIEND ALREADY STRUCK IN SILENCE, AND TAKEN THE SHERIFF'S PLACE, THERE TO LIE IN GHOULISH GLEE UNTIL IT WAS READY TO STRIKE? --A THOUSAND HIDEOUS FANCIES ASSAILED GRISWELL TOOTH AND CLAW.

HE BEGAN TO FEEL THAT HE WOULD GO MAD IF HE DIDN'T LEAP TO HIS FEET, SCREAMING, AND BURST FRENZIEDLY OUT OF THAT ACCURSED HOUSE-- NOT EVEN THE FEAR OF THE GALLOWS COULD KEEP HIM LYING THERE IN THE DARKNESS ANY LONGER! THE RHYTHM OF BUCKNER'S BREATHING WAS SUDDENLY BROKEN, AND GRISWELL FELT AS IF A BUCKET OF ICE-WATER HAD BEEN POURED OVER HIM. FROM SOMEWHERE ABOVE THEM ROSE A SOUND OF WEIRD, SWEET WHISTLING...

GRISWELL'S CONTROL SNAPPED, PLUNGING HIS BRAIN INTO DARKNESS DEEPER THAN THE PHYSICAL BLACKNESS WHICH ENGULFED HIM.

THERE WAS A PERIOD OF ABSOLUTE BLACKNESS, IN WHICH A REALIZATION OF *MOTION* WAS HIS FIRST SENSATION OF AWAKENING CONSCIOUSNESS.

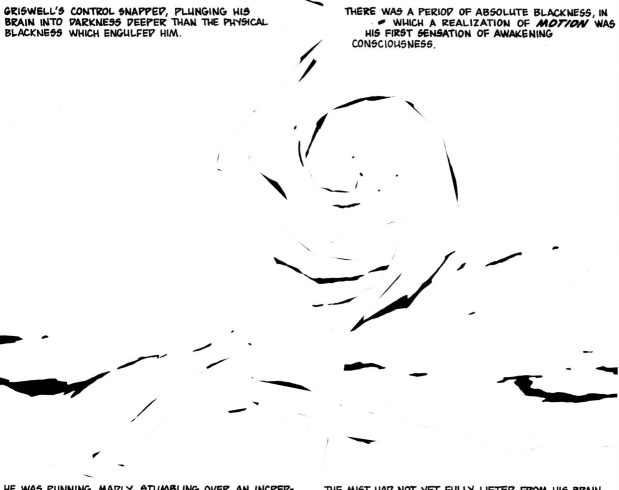

HE WAS RUNNING, MADLY, STUMBLING OVER AN INCREDIBLY ROUGH ROAD. ALL WAS DARKNESS ABOUT HIM, AND HE RAN BLINDLY. VAGUELY HE REALIZED THAT HE MUST HAVE BOLTED FROM THE HOUSE, AND FLED FOR PERHAPS MILES BEFORE HIS OVERWROUGHT BRAIN BEGAN TO FUNCTION. HE DID NOT CARE; DYING ON THE GALLOWS FOR A CRIME HE NEVER COMMITTED DID NOT TERRIFY HIM HALF AS MUCH AS THE THOUGHT OF RETURNING TO THAT HOUSE OF HORROR. HE WAS OVERPOWERED BY THE URGE TO RUN--RUN--RUN AS HE WAS RUNNING NOW, BLINDLY, UNTIL HE REACHED THE END OF HIS ENDURANCE.

THE MIST HAD NOT YET FULLY LIFTED FROM HIS BRAIN, BUT HE WAS AWARE THAT HE COULDN'T SEE THE STARS THROUGH THE BLACK BRANCHES. HE WISHED VAGUELY THAT HE COULD SEE WHERE HE WAS GOING. HE BELIEVED HE MUST BE CLIMBING A HILL, AND THAT WAS STRANGE, SINCE HE KNEW THERE WERE NO HILLS WITHIN MILES OF THE MANOR.

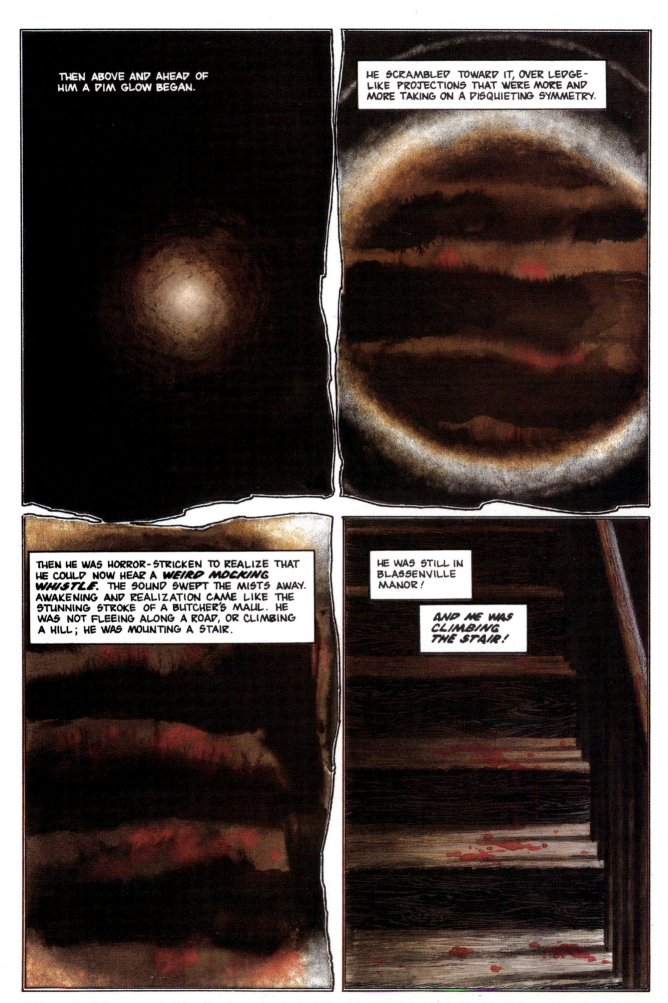

THEN ABOVE AND AHEAD OF HIM A DIM GLOW BEGAN.

HE SCRAMBLED TOWARD IT, OVER LEDGE-LIKE PROJECTIONS THAT WERE MORE AND MORE TAKING ON A DISQUIETING SYMMETRY.

THEN HE WAS HORROR-STRICKEN TO REALIZE THAT HE COULD NOW HEAR A *WEIRD MOCKING WHISTLE.* THE SOUND SWEPT THE MISTS AWAY. AWAKENING AND REALIZATION CAME LIKE THE STUNNING STROKE OF A BUTCHER'S MAUL. HE WAS NOT FLEEING ALONG A ROAD, OR CLIMBING A HILL; HE WAS MOUNTING A STAIR.

HE WAS STILL IN BLASSENVILLE MANOR!

AND HE WAS CLIMBING THE STAIR!

THE MAD WHISTLING ROSE IN A GHOULISH PIPING OF DEMONIC TRIUMPH. HE TRIED TO STOP -- TO TURN BACK -- EVEN TO FLING HIMSELF OVER THE BALUSTRADE, BUT HIS WILL-POWER WAS SHATTERED TO BITS.

HE COULD NOT COMMAND HIS OWN BODY. HIS LEGS, MOVING, WORKED LIKE PIECES OF A MECHANISM DETACHED FROM HIS BRAIN. CLUMPING METHODICALLY THEY CARRIED HIM UP THE STAIR TOWARD THE WITCH-FIRE GLOW SHIMMERING ABOVE HIM.

HE HAD REACHED THE UPPER LANDING AND WAS MOVING DOWN THE LONG HALLWAY. THE WHISTLING SANK, THEN DIED OUT, BUT ITS RESONANCE DROVE HIM ON.

A VAGUE FIGURE WAS SHAMBLING TOWARD HIM. IT LOOKED LIKE A WOMAN, BUT NO HUMAN WOMAN EVER WALKED WITH THAT SKULKING GAIT...

...AND NO HUMAN WOMAN EVER HAD THAT FACE OF *HORROR*, THAT *LEERING BLUR OF LUNACY!* HE TRIED TO SCREAM AT THE SIGHT OF THAT FACE...

...AT THE GLINT OF *KEEN STEEL* IN THE UPLIFTED CLAW-LIKE HAND -- BUT HIS TONGUE WAS *FROZEN.*

AAIIIIIEEE

BLAM! BLAM!

ARE YOU HURT? GOD, MAN, ARE YOU HURT? THERE'S A BUTCHER'S KNIFE...

I'M NOT HURT. YOU FIRED JUST IN TIME. THE *THING!* WHERE IS IT? WHERE DID IT GO?

OVER THERE! I THINK WE MAY HAVE FOUND MISS ELIZABETH'S SECRET PANEL. COME ON.

WHEN THAT WHISTLING STARTED YOU ALMOST WALKED OVER ME GETTIN' OUT. I KNEW YOU WERE HYPNOTIZED OR WHATEVER, SO I FOLLOWED YOU UP THE STAIRS.

I WAS RIGHT BEHIND, BUT CROUCHIN' LOW SO SHE WOULDN'T SEE ME AND MAYBE GET AWAY AGAIN.

I ALMOST WAITED TOO LONG BEFORE I FIRED -- BUT THE SIGHT OF HER ALMOST PARALYZED ME. JESUS!

BUCKNER'S LIGHT BECAME SUDDENLY MOTIONLESS. IN THAT WIDE RING OF LIGHT THREE FIGURES HUNG, THREE DRIED, SHRIVELED, MUMMY-LIKE SHAPES, STILL CLAD IN THE MOLDERING GARMENTS OF THE LAST CENTURY.

THE BLASSENVILLE WOMEN! MISS ELIZABETH WASN'T CRAZY AFTER ALL.

THIS IS WHAT I SAW IN MY DREAM--THE WINDOWLESS CHAMBER, THE BODIES... BUCKNER! LOOK!

WAS THAT THING A WOMAN ONCE?

GOD, LOOK AT THAT FACE, EVEN IN DEATH. LOOK AT THOSE CLAW-LIKE HANDS.

THIS HAS BEEN HER LAIR FOR OVER FORTY YEARS.

THIS CLEARS YOU, GRISWELL-- A CRAZY WOMAN WITH A HATCHET-- THAT'S ALL THE AUTHORITIES NEED TO KNOW.

IT'S STRANGE. JACOB SAID SHE DANCED IN THEIR VOODOO CEREMONIES. HARD TO PICTURE.

JOAN?

UH-UH. WE MISUNDERSTOOD OLD JACOB'S MAUNDERIN'S. JOAN GOT REVENGE, ALRIGHT, BUT NOT AS WE SUPPOSED. SHE DIDN'T DRINK THE BLACK BREW HE MADE FOR HER. IT WAS FOR SOMEBODY ELSE, TO BE GIVEN SECRETLY IN HER FOOD, OR COFFEE, NO DOUBT.

THEN JOAN RAN AWAY LEAVIN' THE SEEDS OF THE HELL SHE SOWED TO GROW.

THAT-- THAT'S NOT THE MULATTO WOMAN?

NOT HARDLY. LOOK AT THE PORTRAIT. HELL, SHE'S EVEN WEARIN' THE SAME DRESS.

FINIS

ROBERT ERVIN HOWARD was born in Peaster, Texas in 1906, and sold his first story to the *Weird Tales* pulp magazine at the age of nineteen, while attending Howard Payne College in Brownwood, Texas. He contributed all sorts of adventure stories to *Weird Tales*, including westerns, sports stories, and fantasy. His robust style soon earned him a great following and he was enormously successful, creating a host of memorable characters such as Solomon Kane and King Kull. Yet it was in 1932 that he gained ever-lasting fame, when he wrote a story entitled "The Phoenix on the Sword," which introduced Conan the Barbarian, the hero against whom all other such heroes have since been judged. Despondent over his mother's impending death, Howard committed suicide in 1936. "Pigeons From Hell," written in 1934, was published posthumously.

SCOTT HAMPTON lives in Columbia, South Carolina and enjoys spending his free time watching horror movies, playing tennis and wallyball, plunking on his guitar, reading, eating out and arguing with his friends and family. He counts among his influences the horror and science fiction comics published by E.C. in the 1950s—which included stories and artwork by Johnny Craig, Al Feldstein, Graham Ingles, Al Williamson, Roy Krenkel, Frank Frazetta, Bernie Krigstein, Reed Crandall, Joe Orlando, Jack Davis, Wally Wood, and George Evans—and those released by Warren Publishing in the 1960s, with stories by Archie Goodwin, and artwork by many of the E.C. artists from a decade before, and also including Alex Toth, Gray Morrow, Dan Adkins, and a particular favorite, Angelo Torres. He also wishes to "extend my thanks to a few generous folks for their time and advice: Mark and Victoria Kneece, Ron and Beverly Jones, George Pratt, Letitia Glozer, Cat Yronwode, Dean Mullaney, Ramsey Campbell, and of course my family."